MATCH WITS WITH

SHERLOCK HOLMES
Volume 8

MATCH WITS WITH
SHERLOCK HOLMES

The Hound
of the Baskervilles

adapted by
MURRAY SHAW
from the original story by Sir Arthur Conan Doyle
illustrated by **GEORGE OVERLIE**

Carolrhoda Books, Inc./Minneapolis

To young mystery lovers everywhere

The author gratefully acknowledges permission granted by Dame Jean Conan Doyle to use the Sherlock Holmes story and characters created by Sir Arthur Conan Doyle.

This book is available in two editions:
Library binding by Carolrhoda Books, Inc.
Soft cover by First Avenue Editions
241 First Avenue North
Minneapolis, MN 55401

Library of Congress Cataloging-in-Publication Data

Shaw, Murray.
    The hound of the Baskervilles / adapted by Murray Shaw from the original story by Sir Arthur Conan Doyle ; illustrated by George Overlie.
        p.   cm. — (Match wits with Sherlock Holmes ; v. 8)
    Summary: An adaptation of one of Doyle's classic mysteries, accompanied by sections identifying clues mentioned in the story.
    ISBN 0-87614-717-1 (lib. bdg.)
    ISBN 0-87614-556-X (pbk.)
    [1. Mystery and detective stories. 2. Literary recreations.]
I. Doyle, Arthur Conan, Sir, 1859-1930. II. Overlie, George, ill.
III. Title. IV. Series: Shaw, Murray. Match wits with Sherlock Holmes ; v. 8.
Pz7.S53726Ho 1993
[Fic]—dc20   92-36133
                                                                CIP
                                                                AC

Manufactured in the United States of America

1 2 3 4 5 6 98 97 96 95 94 93

CONTENTS

INTRODUCTION

In the year 1887, Sir Arthur Conan Doyle created two characters who captured the imagination of mystery lovers around the world. They were Sherlock Holmes—the world's greatest fictional detective—and his devoted companion, Dr. John H. Watson. These characters have never grown old. For over a hundred years, they have delighted readers of all ages.

In the Sherlock Holmes stories, the time is the turn of the 20th century, and the setting, Victorian England. Holmes and Watson live in London, on the second floor of 221 Baker Street. When Holmes travels through back alleys and down gaslit streets to solve crimes, Watson is often at his side. After Holmes's cases are complete, Watson records them. This is the story of the greatest of their adventures.

MORTONHAMPSTEAD

N

Cross

HIGH ROAD

FoulmireFarm

Hut Circles

BASKERVILLE HALL

Berry
Pound

Hut Circles

BLACK TOR

Stone Row

TO COOMBE TRACEY

MERRIPIT
HOUSE

LAFTER HALL

Cairns

Cairn Circle
Cist

HIGH TOR FARM

HIGH TOR

GRIMPEN

Two Stones

Hut Circles

To Ponsworthy

Cairn

Settlement

Map of GRIMPEN
and its surroundings

"He rushed to the window and peered down at
the street, 'Your hat and boots, Watson, quick!' "

THE HOUND
OF THE BASKERVILLES
Part I

It was early on a misty morning in August when Holmes and I were visited by a country doctor from Devonshire. Dr. James Mortimer was a tall, thin man, with a long nose like a beak. Though in his thirties, his back was bowed, and his gold-rimmed spectacles slid down his nose. His keen eyes peered at Holmes intently.

"You interest me very much, Mr. Holmes," said Dr. Mortimer after introductions. "I'm an examiner of skulls, yet I hardly expected you to have such a supra-orbital structure. It is quite extraordinary. A plaster cast of your head would be a find for any museum, until the original is available."

Sherlock Holmes waved our strange visitor to a chair. "I can see, Dr. Mortimer," Holmes said lightly, "that you are as eager a specialist in your interests as I am in mine. But I doubt you came here just to examine my skull."

"No, sir, no," he said, leaning forward in his chair, "though I would be happy to have the opportunity. I came to you, Mr. Holmes, because I face an extraordinary problem, and as you are the second highest expert in Europe—"

"Indeed, sir!" remarked Holmes, bristling. "May I ask who has the honor to be first?"

"Why, to the purely scientific mind, Monsieur Bertillon always appeals most strongly," Dr. Mortimer said sincerely. "But to the practical mind, it is widely known, Mr. Holmes, that you stand alone. I trust I have not offended you."

"Just a little," said Holmes. His curt manner showed he was more than a little offended. "Now, you would do wisely to tell me the problem."

Dr. Mortimer drew a paper from his breast pocket. "I have here a manuscript from the year 1742. It was put in my care by Sir Charles Baskerville, who died most tragically some three months ago. I was his personal friend as well as his doctor. He was a practical man. Yet he took this document seriously and seemed prepared for his abrupt end."

Holmes reached for the manuscript and laid it on his knee. I looked over his shoulder at the yellowed paper and faded script. "It appears to be a legal paper of some sort," said Holmes.

"Yes," agreed the country doctor. "It is an official statement about a legend that runs in the Baskerville family. This manuscript is closely tied to an affair that is far more modern and urgent. The present matter must be decided within twenty-four hours. May I read the statement to you?"

"As you wish," said Holmes. He examined the paper and writing to make sure they were indeed from 1742, and then he handed the sheet to the doctor. Dr. Mortimer read in a high, cracking voice, "This testimony was set down by Richard Baskerville to his sons, Rodger and John:

Many statements have been made regarding the Hound of the Baskervilles. However, since I come in a direct line from Hugo Baskerville and was told the story by my father, I believe the following to be true:

In the 1640s, the time of the Great Rebellion, the Manor of Baskerville was held by Sir Hugo Baskerville. He was known to be a most wild, cruel, and godless man. It chanced that this Hugo came to admire the daughter of a farmer who had lands near the estate. The maiden, knowing his evil reputation, avoided him.

It came to pass that one autumn day, Hugo came down upon the farm with five or six of his wicked companions and carried the maiden away. They brought her to the Hall and locked her in an upper chamber while they feasted. The poor lass was near to having her wits turned from fear. At last, in utter despair, she crawled down the ivy vines that grew up to her window and fled.

Some time later, Hugo left his guests to check on his captive. He found the cage empty and the bird escaped. It was as if the devil entered Hugo then, for he rushed into the dining hall and sprang upon the table. Trenchers and flagons went flying. He cried

that he would give his body to the Powers of Evil if
he could catch the maid.

Then Sir Hugo ran from the Hall, shouting to the
grooms to saddle his horse and unleash the hounds.
He gave the maid's kerchief to the beasts, and they
moved in full cry into the moonlight over the moor.

Thirteen of Hugo's companions took horses and
started in pursuit. The villains had gone but a mile
or two when they passed a shepherd and demanded to
know if he had seen a maiden with the hounds upon
her track. The man was so crazed with fear that he
could scarcely speak. He stuttered that he had. "But
I have seen more than that," the shepherd cried out,
"for Hugo Baskerville passed me upon his black mare.
Behind him ran a gigantic, snarling hound of Hell."
The drunken squires cursed the shepherd and rode
onward. But soon their skins turned cold, for the
black mare came galloping back across the moor toward
them. The horse was dappled with white froth, drag-
ging an empty saddle and a trailing bridle.

A great fear came upon the squires. Only three of
them dared go further. They continued forward slowly until they happened upon the hounds, whimpering
in a pack. The moon was shining bright upon the
clearing, and there in the center stood two great stones
set down by the mysterious people of old. Near the
stones lay the unhappy maid where she had fallen,
dead of fear and exhaustion. But her death did not
raise the hair on the squires' necks. It was the sight
of a great, black beast, shaped like a hound, yet larger

than any hound that a mortal eye has ever rested upon.

As the three men watched, the creature tore the throat out of Sir Hugo Baskerville. Then it turned its blazing eyes and dripping jaws upon them. The men shrieked and rode for dear life. One, it is said, died that very night of what he had seen, and the other two were broken men for the rest of their lives.

Such is the tale, my sons, of the first sighting of the Hound that has so plagued our family. It cannot be denied that many of the family have met unhappy deaths that have been sudden, bloody, and mysterious. Therefore I beg you to trust in the ever goodness of Providence to forgive our family curse. Keep to the good road and avoid the moor in those hours of darkness when the powers of evil are astir.

As Dr. Mortimer finished reading this strange statement, Sherlock Holmes yawned. "Do you not find this legend interesting?" charged Dr. Mortimer.

"To a collector of fairy tales," Holmes remarked.

Dr. Mortimer drew a folded newspaper out of his pocket. "Now then, Mr. Holmes, this article is from the *Devon County Chronicle* of May 14th of this year."

Holmes sat up, and his expression became intent. Our visitor readjusted his spectacles and began:

The sudden death of Sir Charles Baskerville has cast a gloom over the county. The mysterious circumstances of his death have not been entirely cleared up, although there seems no reason to suspect foul play. The facts of the case are simple. On May 4th, Sir Charles declared his intent to start for London the next day, and he promptly ordered his butler, John Barrymore, to prepare his luggage. That night, Sir Charles went out for his usual after-dinner walk. He did not return.

At twelve o'clock, Mr. Barrymore became alarmed and went in search of Sir Charles. The day had been wet, and Barrymore easily traced Baskerville's steps down the manor's famous Yew Alley. Halfway down the path, there is a gate that leads out onto the moor. There were signs that Sir Charles had stood some time at the gate. Then he continued down the alley, away from the house. From his tracks, it appeared that he was tiptoeing.

Barrymore found Sir Charles's body at the far end of the alley. There was no sign of violence, although his face was greatly misshapen from some strong emotion. Sir Charles had not been in the best of health, and his medical adviser, Dr. James Mortimer, suggested that his death could have been from a heart attack. No further information has been uncovered.

In spite of his great wealth, Sir Charles kept a small staff, consisting only of John and Elizabeth Barrymore, the butler and housekeeper; James Perkins, the groom; and Jennifer Heeps, the maid.

The generosity and good cheer of Sir Charles Baskerville will be sorely missed by all. It is hoped that his next of kin, Mr. Henry Baskerville, will carry on Sir Charles's good works in the county.

Dr. Mortimer refolded his paper and pocketed it.

"These are the public facts, Dr. Mortimer," said Holmes, "but I would like some of the private ones."

"I see no reason not to be frank with you, Mr. Holmes," said Dr. Mortimer nervously. "This area of the countryside has few homes, so the people who live here see each other quite often. For that reason, I saw a good deal of Sir Charles. The only others with an education within miles are Mr. Frankland of Lafter Hall, Rodger Stapleton, the naturalist, and Beryl Stapleton, his sister.

"Within the last few months," Dr. Mortimer went on, "it was plain to me that Sir Charles's nervous system was near the breaking point. He had taken the legend of the Hound far too much to heart. Nothing

could entice him to go out onto the moor at night.
One evening a few weeks before his death, I drove
past his home. He chanced to be at the Hall door. As
I walked up, I saw his eyes fix themselves over my
shoulder and stare past me with an expression of the
most dreadful horror. I whisked around and caught
a glimpse of something that appeared to be a large,
black calf passing at the head of the drive. I looked
again, and it was gone."

Dr. Mortimer paused. "It was on this evening,"
he said, "that Sir Charles gave me this statement on
the legend for my safekeeping. At the time, I thought
the event was quite trivial. Therefore, I suggested to
Sir Charles that he take a trip to London to get away
from the gloom that seemed to come to him from the
moor. Mr. Stapleton was in agreement.

"On the night of the tragedy, Barrymore sent the
groom to fetch me. I found the body of Sir Charles
sprawled forward, his fingers dug into the ground. I
could hardly recognize his face, it was so distorted. I
examined the area around the Yew Alley gate but discovered no footprints except Sir Charles's in the soft
ground. However, not far from the body, I saw marks
on the path. . ."

"Footprints?" I asked.

Dr. Mortimer nodded.

"A man's or woman's?" asked Holmes.

Dr. Mortimer looked at us strangely for an instant.
His voice sank almost to a whisper. "They were the
footprints of a gigantic hound!"

I confess these words sent a shudder through me. Holmes leaned forward in his chair, which showed that he, too, was keenly interested. "You saw this?" he probed.

"As clearly as I see you," the doctor responded.

"How was it that no one else saw them?"

"The marks were some twenty yards from the body," the doctor explained, "and no one thought much about them. I should not have cared about them myself had I not known of the legend."

"Are there many sheepdogs on the moor?"

"No doubt there are," the doctor responded, "but this was no sheepdog. The prints were enormous."

"Did they reach the body?" Holmes asked.

"No, they appear to have stopped and turned."

"What is the Yew Alley like?"

"It is a mile-long, private path that passes from the manor house to the summer house at the other end." Dr. Mortimer used his finger to sketch an invisible map on the floor as he spoke. "Six feet of grass and a high hedge of yew shrubs line both sides of the walk. The yews grow so thick and high that nothing can get past or get over them. There is only one opening to the alley other than the summer house and the manor house. It is the gate leading to the moor."

"Had Sir Charles reached the summer house?"

"No, he lay here," he pointed, "about fifty yards from it."

Holmes peered at our guest. "Did the animal prints appear to be coming from the moor gate?"

"Yes. But the gate was closed and padlocked."

"How high is it?"

"About four feet. Anyone could climb over it."

"Did you see any marks by the gate?"

"Only the ones made by Sir Charles. He had stood there for five or ten minutes."

Holmes raised an eyebrow in surprise. "How do you know that?"

"Because I found two mounds of ashes dropped from his cigar. The ashes matched his cigar tobacco."

"Excellent!" cried Holmes. "This is a man after my own heart, Watson." Then Holmes struck his knee in an impatient gesture. "If only I had been there! I might have read so much on the page of that path. Oh, Dr. Mortimer, to think that you should not have called me at once!"

The doctor looked down, wrestling for words. "I couldn't call you in without admitting the facts to the world, rousing up a fear of the old legend. Besides, this may be a case where even the most experienced of detectives is helpless."

"You feel the thing is supernatural?" I asked.

"I do not positively say so, but several people have seen a creature upon the moor that resembles the Baskerville demon. It cannot possibly be an animal known to science. I have cross-examined each person who has seen it. They all agree that it is a huge, black, haunting creature, glowing and ghastly. Every description corresponds with the Hound of legend. Hardly anyone now crosses the moor at night."

"And you," questioned Holmes, "a trained man of science, do you believe it to be supernatural?"

"I don't know what to believe, but it seems that the first Hound was of a devilish nature, yet it still was able to tear out a man's throat."

Holmes shrugged his shoulders. "If you hold these views, then why come to me? How could I possibly assist you?"

"By advising me as to what I should tell Sir Henry Baskerville, who arrives at Waterloo Station"—Dr. Mortimer looked at his watch—"in exactly one hour and a quarter. I speak not as a doctor, but as the person in charge of Sir Charles's will and estate."

"There is no other person claiming the estate, I presume?" Holmes inquired.

"None. Sir Charles had two brothers. His brother Richard died in America as a young man. Richard was the father of this lad, Henry. We found Sir Henry on a farm in Canada. From all accounts, he seems an excellent fellow in every way.

"As for Sir Charles's youngest brother, Rodger Baskerville, he was the black sheep of the family. He was the very image of the family picture of old Hugo. Because of some unsavory dealings, England became too hot for him, and he fled to Central America. There he died in 1876 of yellow fever. He had not married or had children. So far as we can determine, Henry is the last of the Baskervilles. What do you suggest I do with him?"

"Why should he not go on to his family's home?"

"Because the Baskervilles who go there meet an evil fate. I feel sure that Sir Charles would not have wished his nephew to face the same end."

Holmes considered this for a little while. "Put into plain words then," he said, "you believe an actor of a supernatural sort might make Devonshire unsafe for a Baskerville. And yet, if the actor is supernatural, it should be able to work its evil in London as well as in Devonshire, is that not true?"

"You speak more lightly of it, Mr. Holmes, than you would if you had some experience with it. Your advice then is that the young man will be as safe at Baskerville Hall as he would be in London." The thin doctor looked solemnly at Holmes, pushing his spectacles further up his long nose.

"My advice is to take a cab to Waterloo Station to meet Sir Henry," directed Holmes. "Say nothing to him about this affair until I've made up my mind about the matter. Meet me here at ten o'clock tomorrow, and bring Sir Henry Baskerville with you."

"I will do as you say." Dr. Mortimer scribbled the appointment on his shirt cuff with a pencil and hurried out the door in his strange, peering, absent-minded way. Holmes stopped him at the top of the stairs to hand him his walking stick. "One more question, Dr. Mortimer," said Holmes. "You say that several men saw the Hound roaming the moor. Has this been over the last few years or just before Sir Charles's death?"

"Just before his death. I have not heard of any sightings since then."

"Thank you. Good morning, Dr. Mortimer."
Holmes returned to his seat with that quiet look of
inward satisfaction that meant he had an interesting
task ahead of him.

"Going out, Watson?" he asked.

"Not if I can help you here," I replied.

"No, my dear fellow, I turn to you at the hour of
action. If it would be convenient for you to remain
away until evening, I shall then be ready to compare
impressions about the Baskerville dilemma."

I knew that Sherlock depended upon having complete solitude for those hours when he weighed every
particle of evidence. He would construct various the-
ories and balance each against the others. Therefore,
I spent the day at the club and didn't return to Baker
Street until nine o'clock that evening.

As I opened the door, I saw Holmes in his dress-
ing gown, coiled up in his armchair. A rolled map lay
on the table in front of him.

"Good evening, Watson," he said. "You have been
at the club all day, I perceive."

"How did you. . . ?"

Holmes laughed at my bewildered expression. "A
gentleman goes forth on a showery and miry day. He
returns in the evening with the gloss still on his hat
and polish on his boots. Thus, he has been in one
place all day. He is not a man with close friends.
Where, then, could he have been? Is it not obvious,
Watson?"

"Well, yes it is, I suppose."

"The world is full of obvious things that nobody ever observes. Where do you think I have been?"

"Here, no doubt, as is proven by all this smoke."

"On the contrary, my dear Watson, I have been to Devonshire."

"In spirit?"

"Exactly. After you left, I sent down for a county map of this portion of the moor. My body remained in this armchair, but my spirit hovered over the moor. I flatter myself that I could now find my way about."

He unrolled the map and bent over it. "Here is Baskerville Hall, surrounded by woods. There, I fancy, is the Yew Alley, though not marked under that name. This small clump of buildings is the village of Grimpen, where the doctor has his office. Within five miles around, there are only a few scattered dwellings. And here," Holmes said, pointing, "is Lafter Hall, which Dr. Mortimer mentioned. This residence is probably the home of the naturalist, Stapleton, and here are two moorland farmhouses, High Tor and Foulmire. Finally, fourteen miles distant is the prison."

Holmes swept his arm over the map. "This is the stage upon which the tragedy played."

"It must be a wild place."

"Yes. If the devil desires to have his hand in the affairs of humans, this is a worthy spot. But in this case, the devil's agents may be of flesh and blood. Have you turned the case over in your mind, Watson?"

"All day. It's very bewildering."

"There are points of distinction, however," Holmes mused. "That change in Sir Charles's footprints, for instance. What do you make of that?"

"Mortimer said Sir Charles walked on tiptoe."

"He only repeated what some fool had said at the investigation," Holmes said, irritated. "Why should the man walk on tiptoe?"

"What then?"

"He was running, Watson," said Holmes, "running desperately, running for his life, running until his heart burst, and he fell dead upon his face."

"Running from what?"

"There lies our problem. He was clearly crazed with fear before he began to run. He had already told the doctor that he was afraid of the moor. Why would he run *away* from the safety of his house instead of toward it? And why was he waiting at the moor gate for someone on the eve of his trip to London? The thing takes shape, Watson."

Suddenly Holmes uncoiled from his armchair and sat up. "Might I ask you to hand me my violin, Watson? We will postpone all further thoughts upon this business until we have had the advantage of meeting Sir Henry Baskerville."

—— ✐ ——

Our clock had just struck ten when Dr. Mortimer knocked at our chambers, followed by Sir Henry Baskerville. The baronet was a small, alert, dark-eyed man of about thirty years of age. He was sturdily built and had the weather-beaten look of someone who has spent his days in the open air. Something in his steady eye and his quiet, confident manner marked him as a gentleman.

"The strange thing, Mr. Holmes," said Sir Henry after being introduced, "is that if my friend here hadn't proposed coming round to see you, I would have come on my own. I understand you think out little puzzles, and I've had one this morning that needs more thinking than I'm able to give it."

"Pray take a seat, Sir Henry," Holmes said, gesturing to the armchair. "You say you have had some remarkable experience since you arrived in London?"

"Nothing of much importance, Mr. Holmes. Only a joke, probably. It was a letter that reached me this morning." He laid an envelope on the table, and we all bent over it. The address, *Sir Henry Baskerville, Northumberland Hotel*, was printed in rough characters. The postmark was dated the evening before, from the Charing Cross station.

"Who knew you were going to take rooms at the Northumberland?"

"No one could have known. We only decided after I met Dr. Mortimer at the station."

"Hmmm! Someone seems to be deeply interested in your movements, Sir Henry." Holmes slipped a half sheet of paper out of the envelope and spread it on the table. The paper was of common quality and grayish, much like hotel stationery. Across the middle of it was a sentence formed by individual words clipped from a newspaper. The message ran:

The word "moor" was printed in black ink.

"Now," said Sir Henry, "perhaps you will tell me, Mr. Holmes, what in heaven's name is the meaning of that, and who seems to take such an interest in my affairs?"

Holmes gestured to me. "Do you have yesterday's *Times* with you, Watson?"

The paper was in the corner, within reach, and I passed it over to him. Holmes glanced swiftly over it and then read aloud from a front-page article:

You may imagine that your industry will be encouraged by a protective tariff, but it stands to reason that such tariffs will in the long run decrease the value of

*our trade and lower the general conditions of life on
this island as it shall keep away wealth from the country.*

"What do you think of that, Watson?" cried Holmes
in high glee, rubbing his hands together with great
satisfaction.

Dr. Mortimer and Sir Henry turned puzzled eyes
on me. "I don't know about tariffs," said the baronet
in a feisty tone, "but it seems we've gotten a bit off
the trail."

"On the contrary," Holmes stated, "I think we're hot
upon it. Watson knows more about my methods than
you do, Sir Henry, but I fear even he hasn't yet grasped
the importance of this sentence. Note the words: *You,
your, life, and, reason, value, as, keep away,* and *from
the.* Don't you see from whence these words came?"

"By thunder, you're right!" cried Sir Henry. "Well,
if that isn't smart!"

"To prove the truth of my theory, note that *keep
away* and *from the* were both cut out in one piece,"
Holmes pointed out.

"Well, now—so they were!" Dr. Mortimer gazed
at my friend in amazement. "How did you do it?"

"Newspapers and their printed type are my special
hobbies. Any trained crime specialist knows the dif-
ferences between type styles. Since I read the *Times*
daily, I recognized the print immediately. This note
was posted yesterday, so it seemed likely that the
words were cut from yesterday's issue. Thus it was
merely a matter of finding the correct paragraph."

"But why was the word *moor* handwritten?" asked Sir Henry.

"Because the sender could not find it in print. The ink splattering in the address, the carelessly pasted words, and the sloppiness of the clippings show that the author of this note was probably in a hurry. Perhaps this person feared being caught in the act."

"Why, of course, that would explain it. Do you read anything else in this message, Mr. Holmes?"

"The *Times* is a paper usually read by people who are highly educated. I believe the letter was composed by an educated person who wishes to appear uneducated. Now, Sir Henry, has anything else of particular interest happened to you since you've been in London?"

"Why, no, I think not."

"You have not observed anyone following or watching you?"

"I seem to have walked right into the thick of a dime novel," Sir Henry remarked, puzzled. "Why in thunder should anyone follow or watch me?"

"We are coming to that. Nothing else to report?"

"Well, it depends upon what you think is worth reporting. But I hope that losing one of your boots is not part of ordinary life over here."

"You've lost one of your boots?"

"My dear sir," cried Dr. Mortimer, sounding slightly embarrassed, "it is only mislaid. It will no doubt be there when you return to the hotel."

"Well, Mr. Holmes asked for anything outside the

ordinary routine," exclaimed Sir Henry.

"Exactly," said Holmes. "However foolish it may seem. You have lost one of your boots, you say?"

"Well, mislaid it, anyhow. I put both outside my door to be cleaned last night, and there was only one there this morning. I could get no sense out of the chap who cleans them. The worst of it is I only bought the pair last night. I've never even had them on."

"If you never wore them, why did you put them out to be cleaned?"

"They hadn't been sealed against water. So I put them out for varnish."

"A new boot does seem to be a singularly useless thing to steal," said Sherlock Holmes. "I confess that I share Dr. Mortimer's belief that the missing boot will be returned before long."

"It seems to me," said the baronet with decision, "that now is the time that you give me a full accounting of what you are both driving at."

"Your request is only reasonable," said Holmes. "Dr. Mortimer, it would be best for you to tell your story as you told it to us."

Thus, our scientific friend, Dr. Mortimer, drew his papers from his pocket and presented the whole case as he had done the morning before. Baskerville listened with deep attention and an occasional exclamation of surprise.

"Well," Sir Henry said, "of course, I've heard of the Hound ever since I was in the nursery. But as to my uncle's death, you don't seem to have made up your mind whether it's a case for a policeman or a clergyman. And now there's this letter. I suppose that fits into place somewhere."

"It shows someone knows more than we do about what's going on upon the moor," said Dr. Mortimer.

"What we must now decide, Sir Henry," said Holmes, "is whether or not you should travel on to Baskerville Hall."

"Why should I not go? Do you fear danger from the family fiend or from human beings?"

"That is precisely what we intend to find out," said Holmes.

Sir Henry's dark brows knitted over his nose, and his face flushed to a dusky red. It was obvious that the fiery temper of the Baskervilles was not yet extinct. "No devil in Hell or man on earth can prevent me from going to the home of my own people," spouted the baronet. "In the meantime, I have hardly had time to think out all you have told me. This is a big thing for a man to have to understand and then decide upon a plan of action in one sitting. I would like a quiet hour to think." Glancing at his watch, he added, "It's half past eleven now. Why not come and have lunch with me at two o'clock at the hotel?"

Holmes turned to me. "Is that convenient for you, Watson?"

"Perfectly."

"Then you may expect us," said Holmes. "Shall I call a cab?"

"I'd prefer to walk," responded Sir Henry. "This affair has rather flurried me."

"I'll join you," said Dr. Mortimer.

As soon as they left, Holmes changed from a sluggish listener to a man of action. He rushed to the window and peered down at the street. "Your hat and boots, Watson, quick! Not a moment to lose!"

We threw on our coats and flew down the stairs. Dr. Mortimer and Sir Henry could be seen about two hundred yards ahead of us on the street.

"Shall I run on and stop them?" I asked.

"Not for the world, Watson. It's a fine morning for a walk."

We followed them at a distance. Once, our friends stopped and stared into a shop window. Holmes and I did the same. Sir Henry and Dr. Mortimer started to walk again, and a hansom cab on the opposite side of the street began moving slowly after the baronet and the doctor. Holmes gave a cry of satisfaction.

"There's our man, Watson! Come along! We'll have a good look at him, if we can do no more."

A bushy black beard and a pair of piercing eyes turned upon us through the side window of the cab. Instantly, the trapdoor at the top of the cab flew up, and something was shouted at the driver. The cab flew off madly down the street.

Holmes looked around for a cab to follow it, but no empty cab was in sight. He dashed through the heavy traffic in wild pursuit. The cab drove out of sight around a curve.

My friend returned, panting and white. "There, now!" cried Holmes, bitterly, "Was there ever such bad luck and management?"

"Who was that man?" I asked, confused.

"I have no idea."

"A spy?"

"Indeed. It was clear that Sir Henry has been shadowed ever since he's been in town. How else could it be so quickly known that he was staying at the Northumberland Hotel?"

"Holmes," I said, "I do not know how you could have done better in trying to follow the man."

"By too much haste and eagerness, I betrayed myself and lost our man."

"What a pity, then," I moaned, "that we did not get the number of the cab!"

"My dear Watson," said Holmes, "clumsy as I have been, surely you do not imagine that I neglected to get the number—2704 is our man. Could you swear to that man's face in the cab?"

"Only to the beard."

"That is my thought," said Holmes. "Therefore, I gather that it was probably a false one. Now we must find something to occupy ourselves until lunch."

———— ∽ ————

At the Northumberland Hotel, we came round the top of the stairs and ran up against Sir Henry himself. "Seems to me someone in this hotel is playing me for a fool," he yelled, his face flushed with anger. In one of his hands was an old dusty boot. "If that chap can't find my missing boot, there will be trouble. I can take a joke with the best of them, but this is a bit over the mark."

"Still looking for your boot?" I asked.

"Now it's a different one—an old black one," he replied, sputtering in fury. "I had only three pairs of boots: the new brown ones, the old black, and the patent leathers I'm wearing. Yesterday they sneaked one of the brown ones, and today they snatched one of the black!"

A nervous old waiter came up the stairs.

"Well, have you got it?" cried Sir Henry. "Speak out, man, and don't stand staring!"

The waiter cringed. "No, sir. I've asked all over the hotel, but I hear no word of it."

"Either that boot comes back before sundown, or I'll see the manager."

The waiter bowed. "It shall be found, sir, if you'll have a little patience."

"Mind that it is, for it's the last thing I'll lose here," barked Sir Henry. Then he turned to Holmes and said in a calmer voice, "Mr. Holmes, you must excuse my troubling you about such a trifle."

"I think it's well worth troubling about."

"Why, you look very serious about it. What do you make of it, Mr. Holmes?"

"I don't profess to understand it yet," he replied. "This case cuts deep. But we hold several threads in our hands, and one of them may guide us to the truth."

We sat down to a pleasant luncheon in a private dining chamber. Little was said about what had brought us together. Later, Holmes asked Sir Henry what he intended to do.

"I have some business to finish here. I'll go to Baskerville Hall at the end of the week."

"I think your decision is wise, Sir Henry. You are being dogged here, and amid all the people in this great city, it's difficult to discover who is responsible. If someone means you harm, we should be unable to prevent it."

"I'm being followed? By whom?"

"I cannot tell you that at present. Dr. Mortimer, have you any neighbors with a full black beard?"

"Barrymore, Sir Charles's butler, has one. He lives at the Hall."

"We had best make sure he is really there then, or if by chance he is in London. Take the telegram form, Dr. Mortimer. Write a quick note saying, *Is all ready for Sir Henry?* Address this to *Mr. Barrymore, Baskerville Hall, Grimpen*. You will send a second wire to the postmaster at Grimpen saying, *Telegram to Mr. Barrymore to be delivered into his own hand. If absent, please return wire to Sir Henry Baskerville, Northumberland Hotel*. That should let us know before evening whether Barrymore is at his post or not."

"Dr. Mortimer," asked the baronet, "what do you know of this butler?"

"He has looked after the Hall for some time. So far as I know, he and his wife are respectable people."

"Did Barrymore gain any money from Sir Charles's will?" Holmes inquired.

"He and his wife received five hundred pounds each. But Sir Charles included everyone he could in his will. I hope that does not make us all suspects. For I received a thousand pounds as well."

"Indeed!" cried Holmes. "Who else?"

"A large amount went to charities. The leftover went to Sir Henry—740,000 pounds."

Holmes raised his eyebrows in surprise. "I had no idea so great a sum was involved."

"We knew Sir Charles was rich," said Dr. Mortimer, "but we had no idea how rich. The total value of the estate was close to a million."

"Dear me!" said Holmes. "A man might well play a desperate game for so much. Who would inherit the estate if anything happened to Sir Henry?"

"Sir Charles's youngest brother died unmarried, so the estate would pass to James Desmond. He is a distant cousin, who is an elderly clergyman in Westmoreland," explained Dr. Mortimer.

"Have you met him?"

"Yes. He seems a most saintly man," said the doctor. "He refused to accept any money from Sir Charles before or after his death."

"Have you made your will, Sir Henry?"

"No, Mr. Holmes. I've had no time."

"Well, Sir Henry," stated my companion, "I advise you to go to Devonshire without delay. But you must not go alone. Since Dr. Mortimer must return to his practice, you must take with you a trusty man who will not leave your side."

"Whom would you recommend?"

Holmes laid his hand upon my arm. "Since I have cases to finish up, I cannot be there, except in the case of an emergency. However, if my friend, Dr. Watson, would undertake it, there is no better man."

Before I had time to answer, Sir Henry seized me by the hand and wrung it heartily. "Well, now, that is very kind of you, Dr. Watson," said he. "If you come down to Baskerville Hall and see me through this, I'll never forget it."

The promise of adventure always fascinated me, and I was complimented by Holmes's words. "I will come with pleasure," said I.

"And you will report closely to me," said Holmes.

"When a crisis comes, as it must, I will direct you how to act. Now, then, would you all be prepared to leave by Saturday?"

"Certainly," was our response.

"I suggest the three of you take the ten-thirty train from Paddington Station."

With this decided, Holmes and I accompanied Sir Henry down the hall to his private chambers. When he opened the door, he gave a cry of triumph. He dove into one of the corners of the room and drew out a brown boot from under a cabinet. "My missing boot!" he cried. "The waiter must have placed it here while we were having lunch."

He called the waiter, but the man did not know anything about it. Nor did anyone else.

As we drove back to Baker Street, Holmes sat in silence. I was sure he was trying to frame some scheme into which all these strange, disconnected bits of information could fit. All afternoon and late into the evening, he sat lost in thought.

Just before dinner, a telegram was delivered. It ran: *Barrymore is at the Hall—Baskerville*

"There goes one of our leads!" proclaimed Holmes. "We must cast around for another scent."

"We have the cabman who drove the spy," I noted.

"Exactly. I have wired to get his name and address from the Official Registry." Just then, the bell rang. "I should not be surprised if this were an answer to my question." Holmes opened the door to display a rough-looking fellow who was obviously the very cabman himself. "The head office said that you've been asking about Number 2704," he said angrily. "I've driven my cab seven years and never had a complaint. I'm here to ask you what you got against me."

"My good man, I've nothing against you," Holmes said, his voice serene. "On the contrary, I have half a sovereign for you if you give me a clear answer to my questions."

"Well, I've had a good day and no mistake," said the cabman with a grin. "What was it you wanted to ask, sir?"

"First of all, your name and address, in case I want you again."

"John Clayton, 3 Turpey Street."

Holmes noted it. "Now, Mr. Clayton," he said, "tell me about the passenger who watched this house and then followed two gentlemen down Regent Street."

The man looked surprised and a little embarrassed. "Why, the gentleman told me he was a detective and that I was to say nothing to anyone."

"He told you he was a detective?"

"Yes, he did."

"Now, my good fellow, you could find yourself in a bad position if you try to hide anything from me. Did he say anything else?"

"He mentioned his name."

Holmes cast a quick triumphant look at me. "Oh, he mentioned his name, did he? That was foolish. What name did he give you?"

"His name," exclaimed the cabman, "was Sherlock Holmes."

Never have I seen my friend more completely taken aback. For an instant, he sat in amazement. Then he burst into a hearty laugh.

"A distinct touch, Watson!" he cried. "I feel a sword as sharp as my own. So his name was Sherlock Holmes, was it? Tell me where you picked him up and all that occurred."

"He hailed me in Trafalgar Square. Told me he was a detective and offered me money if I did exactly what he wanted all day without questions. First, we drove down to the Northumberland Hotel and waited there until two gentlemen came out and took a cab. We followed their cab until it pulled up near here."

"To this very door."

"I can't say. We pulled up halfway down the street and waited an hour and a half. Then the two men passed us. We followed them down Baker Street until we got partway down Regent Street. Then my passenger cried that I should drive straight away to Waterloo Station as hard as I could go. I whipped up the horses and was there in under ten minutes."

"How would you describe this Sherlock Holmes?"

The cabman scratched his head. "I'd put him at forty years of age; middle height, about three inches shorter than you, sir. He had a black beard, square cut, and a pale face. That's about all, sir."

"Well, then, here is your half sovereign, Mr. Clayton. Good night."

"Good night, sir." He departed chuckling.

Holmes turned to me with a troubled smile. "Snap goes our third thread," said he. "The cunning rascal knew our number—he knew that Sir Henry had talked to me, so he sent back his insultingly bold message. I tell you, Watson, we have a foe worthy of our steel. I'm uneasy about sending you to Devonshire. It's an ugly, dangerous business. Yes, my dear Watson, you may laugh, but I shall be very glad to have you back safe and sound in Baker Street."

Holmes and Watson have tracked down one lead after another, but where have the clues led them? Are they dealing with the demon Hound or a cunning human? Or both? Keep close on their trail, and look over the **Clues** *to make sure you are matching wits with the greatest detective of all time on his greatest case.*

CLUES
that will lead to the solution of
The Hound of the Baskervilles

Sir Charles was afraid of the moor, yet he stood around at the gate. Whom was he waiting to meet? Why hadn't he told anyone about the meeting? Whoever set up the meeting probably knows something about Sir Charles's death.

Dr. Mortimer found some paw prints near Sir Charles's body. If the animal can make a paw print, it must be real and not just a legend. Something about it was so frightening that Sir Charles ran to his death. Where did it come from and where did it go? Why was it only seen right before Sir Charles's death and not since? Holmes will have to track this hound.

the MOOR Holmes figured out that someone was following Sir Henry, because the warning note was sent to the correct hotel. The words were taken from the *Times*, which is a newspaper that is read by well-educated people. The letter may be a threat or a well-intended warning. Is Dr. Mortimer as true a friend as he seems? The note was made in a hurry, as if the sender was afraid of being discovered. Is more than one person involved?

Dr. Mortimer said the butler, Barrymore, had a full, black beard. Holmes suspected that the beard he saw on the stranger in the cab was a disguise, but he wanted to follow up on every clue. By sending a telegram to Barrymore, Holmes was able to discover that the butler was not in London. So he deduced that someone else is pretending to be Sherlock Holmes.

"As we approached, a tall young man with
a dark beard stepped from the shadow of the porch."

THE HOUND
OF THE BASKERVILLES
Part II

t the appointed time, Sherlock Holmes drove
with me to the station. As he saw us off on the
train, Holmes requested that I write to him and report
the facts in the fullest possible manner. He also
reminded me to keep Sir Henry Baskerville continually in sight. Then he warned Sir Henry to remember
the legend and to "avoid the moor in those hours of
darkness when the powers of evil are astir."

The journey to Devonshire was a swift and pleasant one. Sir Henry cried aloud with delight as he
caught sight of places he remembered from childhood
before his father's death. "I've been over a good part
of the world, Dr. Watson, but I never saw a place to
compare with Devonshire."

The green squares of fields and the dark, curving
woods flashed past the train window. As time went
on, gray hills with strange, jagged edges rose in the distance, like some fantastic landscape in a dream. This
was the boggy moorland where so many nightmares
had occurred.

The train pulled up at a small, wayside station.
Two men in uniforms stood leaning against their short
rifles near the gate. This struck me as unusual for such
a sweet, simple country spot, but I had not long to

think about it. Perkins, the Baskerville Hall groom, was waiting for us in a small wagon. He was a hard-faced, gnarled little fellow. Soon we were flying swiftly down the road.

As we came to the top of one of the gray hills, we spotted a mounted soldier. Perkins half-turned in his seat. "A convict escaped from the Princeton prison, sir," said he. "The soldiers are looking for him on every road. He's been out three days now, but no sign of him yet. He's no ordinary convict. He's Selden, the Notting Hill murderer. People hereabouts worry about getting their throats cut."

We all fell silent, and Sir Henry pulled his overcoat more closely around him. We kept moving down the road until two high, narrow towers thrust up over the twisted trees. Perkins pointed his whip and called, "Baskerville Hall."

At the far end of the long drive, the house glimmered like a ghost in the sinking sun. The Hall was a ruin of black granite and old wooden ribs, with a new building hanging alongside.

"It's no wonder my uncle felt trouble coming down on him in such a place," the young baronet said. "I'll have a row of electric Edison lights put up around the outside within six weeks."

As we approached, a tall, young man with a dark beard stepped from the shadow of the porch. "Welcome to Baskerville Hall, Sir Henry!" A woman stepped out from behind the man to help him with the bags. These were the Barrymores.

We unloaded the wagon, and Dr. Mortimer excused himself, so that he might return to his own home and wife. Then Sir Henry and I entered the Hall, and the heavy door clanged shut behind us. We gazed around us at the high, thin windows of stained glass, the oak paneling, and the coat of arms upon the wall. Sir Henry's face lit up with boyish enthusiasm.

Barrymore stepped up behind us. "Dinner will be ready in a few moments, sir. I wish to say that my wife and I will be happy to stay on until you find other help."

"You mean to say that you wish to leave?" asked Sir Henry. "But your family has worked for us for generations."

The young butler's handsome face twisted with some emotion. "We were attached to Sir Charles, and his death gave us quite a shock. We will never again feel quite at ease here, I fear. Through Sir Charles's generosity, we will be able to set up some business of our own."

He left us, and we stepped into the dining room. It was a place of shadow and gloom. From the high, dark walls, portraits of ancestors stared mournfully down upon us.

"My word," said Sir Henry after we had eaten. "It isn't a very cheerful place. Perhaps things will look brighter in the morning."

A double stairway took us to our rooms along a corridor on a long gallery. Mine was in the same wing as Baskerville's, almost next door. Before I went to bed, I looked out my window. Two stands of trees moaned and swung in the rising wind. I lay down, weary but wakeful. The time passed painfully slowly, and I listened to the chiming clock strike as the quarter hours passed. Suddenly there came to my ears the unmistakable sound of a woman sobbing, torn by an uncontrollable sorrow. I sat up, listening intently. For half an hour I waited, every nerve on the alert. But there came no other sound, save the chiming of the distant clock.

As Sir Henry and I sat at breakfast, the fresh beauty of the morning streamed through the high windows of the dining room. The gloom of last night had lifted.

"I guess it is ourselves and not the house we have to blame!" said the baronet cheerfully.

"And yet, Sir Henry, I heard a woman sobbing in the night. Did you?"

"It's curious, but I did hear something of the sort. But there was no more of it, so I concluded it was a dream. Since you heard it too, we must ask about it right away."

He rang the bell and asked Barrymore whether he could explain our experience. The butler's pale features turned a shade lighter. "There are two women in the house, Sir Henry. One is the maid. The other is my wife. The sobs did not come from her."

Later, though, when I met Mrs. Barrymore, her eyes were red and swollen. No doubt it was she who had been weeping. Why? And why had her husband lied about her tears?

That morning, while Sir Henry stayed at home to work on some papers, I visited the postmaster. To my dismay, I discovered that Sherlock's telegram had been given to Mrs. Barrymore, not to her husband. There was still no proof that John Barrymore had been at the Hall to receive it. Holmes's clever trick had failed to flush the bird.

As I walked along the gray, lonely road back to Baskerville Hall, I wondered if Barrymore had killed

Sir Charles or tried to scare Sir Henry away. I hoped that my friend might soon be freed from his responsibilities and be able to come down to take this heavy burden off my shoulders. Then from behind me, I heard running feet and a voice calling my name. I turned, expecting to see Dr. Mortimer.

To my surprise, it was a stranger. He was small, slim, clean shaven, blond-haired, and lean jawed. Between thirty and forty years old, he wore a straw hat and carried a butterfly net and tin box. "You will excuse my bursting upon you so suddenly, Dr. Watson," said he, panting. "Here we folks don't

wait for introductions. I am Rodger Stapleton of
Merripit House. Our good Dr. Mortimer may have
spoken of me."

"Your net and box would have told me you were the
naturalist. But how did you know me?"

"Dr. Mortimer pointed you out from his window,"
said Stapleton. "How is Sir Henry? He must be of
sturdy mind to choose to live at the Hall after the
mysterious manner of Sir Charles's death. He has no
superstitions then?"

"It doesn't seem likely. Why?" I asked.

"You must have heard about the fiend dog that is
thought to roam the moor?" Stapleton chattered on.
"The local farmers have taken hold of this story, and
any number would swear they have seen it. Sir Charles
quite feared the Hound, and dogs in general, and that
may have led to his tragic end."

"You think that some dog chased Sir Charles and
he died of fright?"

"Dr. Mortimer told me that the old man had a frail
heart. I think that any farmer's dog that passed outside the property might have scared him to death.
Have you heard any better explanation?"

"I have not come to any conclusion," I admitted.

"Has Sherlock Holmes?"

I was quite shocked that Stapleton would have
known of Holmes. My surprise must have shown.
He chuckled, "Ah, Dr. Watson, we are country folk,
but even we have read your records of the celebrated
Sherlock Holmes. Since you are here, it follows that

Mr. Holmes is interesting himself in this matter. As a man of science, I'm curious to know what view of the matter he takes."

"I'm afraid I don't know. Mr. Holmes is busy at present and can't leave London. I'm simply here to pay a visit to my friend, Sir Henry."

"Excellent!" cried Stapleton. Then he pointed to a path that veered off and climbed a granite bluff overlooking the moor. "A walk along this path brings us to Merripit House. Perhaps you can spare an hour to meet my sister."

My first thought was that I should be by Sir Henry's side. Yet I knew he was tied up by a stack of papers, and Holmes had expressly said that I should study the neighbors. So I accepted the naturalist's invitation, and we turned together down the path. "Do you know the moor well?" I inquired.

"I've only been here two years," he said. "But my tastes have led me to explore every part of the country round, and I think few men know it better than I."

Stapleton paused and looked out over the rolling green hills and sighed. "It's a wonderful place, the moor. You see that great plain with the hills breaking out of it? Do you notice anything remarkable about it?"

"It would be a rare place for a gallop."

"You would naturally think so," he explained, "and that thought has cost several people their lives. That plain is the great Grimpen Mire. You notice those bright green spots scattered over it? One false step,

Dr. Watson, means death to human or beast. Only yesterday I saw one of the moor ponies wander into it. I heard a long, mournful cry, and the bog hole sucked him up. It's a bad place, the Grimpen Mire. Yet I can find my way through the heart of it."

"You can?"

"Yes," boasted Stapleton. "One or two paths wind amongst the bog holes. They lead to the hills beyond. Those hills are really islands, and that's where the rare butterflies are, if you have the wits to reach them."

"Halloa!" I cried. "What is that?"

A long, low moan, incredibly sad, swept over the moor. It was impossible to tell where it had started. From a dull murmur, it swelled into a deep roar, and then sank back. Stapleton looked at me with a queer expression on his face.

"The farmers round here say that's the Hound of the Baskervilles calling for its next victim. I've heard it before, but never quite so loud."

I looked around with a chill in my heart. "You are an educated man," I said. "You don't believe such nonsense, do you? What do you think was the cause of that sound?"

"It may have been the mud settling, or the water rising, or even the call of a bird known as the bittern. The moor is a strange place, there's no denying it. Look over at the hills yonder," Stapleton said, pointing. "The stone huts upon them were once the homes of prehistoric people. They can give one an eerie feeling. Ah, there's a beauty!"

A small moth had fluttered across our path, and in an instant, Stapleton had sped off in pursuit. The creature flew straight down the bluff and over the great mire. My companion never paused, bounding from tuft to tuft, his green net waving in the air.

As I watched his pursuit, a young woman rounded a corner in the path ahead. She came from the direction of the Merripit House. No doubt, she was Miss Stapleton. Yet the contrast between the sister and brother could not have been greater. Her hair and eyes were darker than those of any woman I've seen in England. In her elegant dress, the slim woman was a strange sight upon a lonely moorland path. She quickened her pace toward me.

"Go back!" she commanded. "Go straight back to London instantly!"

I could only stare at her in stupid surprise. "Why should I go back?"

"I cannot explain," she said, her eyes blazing. "Don't you know when a warning is for your own good? For God's sake, do what I ask of you. Hush, my brother is coming back. Not a word to him of what I said."

Stapleton had abandoned his chase and was climbing the hill back to us, flushed from the run. "Halloa, Beryl!" he called, though it seemed that his greeting was not altogether friendly. "You have introduced yourselves, I see."

"Yes," the woman said, smiling politely, "I was just telling Sir Henry that it is rather late for him to see orchids, the true beauties of the moor."

"Well, we had not quite introduced ourselves," I explained. "I am only a humble commoner—Dr. John Watson, a friend of Sir Henry's."

"Ah, excuse me," said Miss Stapleton, somewhat embarrassed. "It seems we have been talking at cross purposes. I was so proud of our orchids that I made a silly assumption. But will you not walk on, Dr. Watson, and see Merripit House?"

"Indeed," said her brother, "that was our destination."

A short walk brought us to a bleak moorland house that had been turned into a modern dwelling. Inside, there were large rooms and elegant furnishings. I could not but marvel at what could have brought this highly educated man and woman to this place.

"Queer spot to choose, is it not?" said Stapleton, as if in answer to my thoughts. I nodded, and he explained, "I had a school in the north country, but unfortunately, the flu hit us there, and three boys died. We shut down the school and moved here. There is endless fieldwork to do here, and my sister is as devoted to nature as I am. We have our books and our studies and interesting neighbors. We are quite happy, aren't we, Beryl?"

"Quite happy," said she, but her voice had no vigor.

"We miss Sir Charles, it is true. But we are eager to be introduced to the new baronet. Do you think we could call on Sir Henry this afternoon?"

"I'm sure he would be delighted."

"Now, Dr. Watson, if you are interested, I could show you my special collection of rare butterflies."

Since it was getting quite late, I decided to save his invitation for another time. I set off at once upon my return journey, taking the path by which we had come.

There must have been some shortcut, for I came upon Miss Stapleton waiting for me on a rock by the path. Her breath was short, and her beautiful face was pink from effort.

"I ran all the way to cut you off, Dr. Watson. I'm sorry for the silly mistake I made. Please forget my words. They do not apply to you."

"But I cannot forget them, Miss Stapleton. Please tell me what you meant," I insisted.

A questioning expression passed over her face for an instant. Then her eyes hardened. "You make too much of it, Dr. Watson. Because of Sir Charles's unexplained death, I could only fear for Sir Henry.

The world is so wide. It seems strange that Sir Henry would want to live in Baskerville Hall with such a strange and terrifying legend hanging about it."

"If this is what has been bothering you, Miss Stapleton, why were you reluctant to have your brother know your thoughts?"

"My brother wants us to have a new neighbor, and he wouldn't want me to scare Sir Henry away. But I felt it was my duty, and now I will say no more. I must get back before my brother suspects where I am. Good-bye!" She turned and disappeared among the large, scattered boulders.

With my soul full of vague fears, I made my way back to Baskerville Hall.

— ⌘ —

For the next few weeks, I sent short telegrams to Holmes to keep him up-to-date. Finally, by October 13th, I had enough new information to send Holmes a full report, which ran as follows:

My dear Holmes,

The longer one stays here, the more the spirit of the moor sinks into one's soul. The convict who escaped from prison still has not been captured. It is thought he is hiding out on the moor, possibly in the prehistoric stone huts there. I am uneasy about the Stapletons living so far from help. All in the household would be helpless in the hands of the Notting Hill murderer.

Sir Henry is beginning to display a great interest in the lovely Miss Stapleton. Her brother came to call upon Baskerville the first day, and the next morning he showed us the spot where the legend of the wicked Hugo took place—it was at a ring of ancient stones near the stone huts. Afterward, we stayed for lunch at Merripit House. It was then that Sir Henry met Miss Stapleton. From the first, he was attracted to her, and she seems to feel the same. Since then, hardly a day has passed when we have not seen the brother and sister. If this love affair continues, I may not be able to keep a close watch on Sir Henry when he goes out.

I would have thought Rodger Stapleton would welcome the match. Yet he casts strong looks of disapproval whenever Sir Henry pays attention to his sister. No doubt Stapleton would feel quite lonely without her.

Dr. Mortimer comes to see us nearly every day. He talks about the shapes of skulls and local gossip. I had the occasion to meet another neighbor—Mr. Frankland of Lafter Hall, four miles to the south. He is an elderly man—red-haired, white-faced, and bitter. He has spent a fortune suing people, sometimes for practically no reason. Being an amateur astronomer, Frankland has set up an excellent telescope on his roof, and he sweeps his eyes over the moor all day in hopes of catching sight of the escaped criminal.

As for the butler at Baskerville Hall, Barrymore insists that he was working in the loft when your telegram was delivered to him by his wife. Sir Henry

questioned him, until Barrymore cried out, "Have I
done something that makes you distrust me?" He was
so upset that Sir Henry finally gave the butler his old
American clothes as a gift to assure him of his trust.
As for Mrs. Barrymore, I have more than once noticed
traces of tears on her face. Perhaps some deep sorrow lies hidden.

Last night, at about two in the morning, I was
awakened by a slow step passing my room. I rose,
opened the door, and peeped out. A man was moving down the passage with bare feet and a candle in
hand. Because of his height, I was sure it was
Barrymore. There was something indescribably guilty
about him.

I waited until he passed round the corner and then
followed him. When I turned the corner, I saw he had

entered one of the unused rooms. I looked in and saw Barrymore crouching with the candle held against the window. He stared out at the blackness of the moor. Then with a deep groan, he put out the light. Instantly, I turned and made my way back to my room. A while afterward, I heard a key turn downstairs in one of the outer doors.

What it all means, I cannot guess. But there is some mysterious, secret, black business going on in this house of gloom. I had a long talk with Sir Henry, and we made a plan. I will speak about it more in my next report.

— ✑ —

October 15

My dear Holmes,

Since my last report, things have taken an unexpected turn. I examined the room in which Barrymore had been. I noticed that the window commands the clearest sight of the moor. The butler must have been looking out for something or someone on the moor. It occurred to me that he might be waiting for a young woman. This might be why his wife is so bothered by grief.

When I told Sir Henry about the butler's nightly adventure, he was not surprised. He had heard stirrings in the house during the night. "I suggest," said the baronet, "that we sit up in my room tonight and wait until he passes. Then we'll follow him and see what he does."

We had an entire day, however, before our plan could be carried out. Sir Henry put on his hat and prepared to go out. As a matter of duty, I did the same. Sir Henry put his hand on my shoulder with a pleasant smile. "My dear fellow," said he, "I'm sure you are the last man who would wish to be a spoilsport. I must go out alone."

This put me in an awkward position. Before I had made up my mind what to do, he picked up his cane and was gone. Imagine my feelings if some misfortune fell upon Sir Henry while I disregarded your instructions. So I set out at once in the direction of Merripit House.

I mounted a hill, and then I saw him below with Miss Stapleton at his side. They were deeply absorbed in conversation. Sir Henry put his hand around the woman's shoulders, and suddenly Rodger Stapleton appeared, running wildly toward them. He waved his arms violently and almost danced with excitement in front of the lovers. I couldn't hear what he was saying, but he seemed angry with the couple. Then the naturalist left, pulling his sister along. Sir Henry hung his head and walked slowly back the way he had come.

I met the baronet at the bottom of the hill. "Halloa, Watson!" he called. "Where have you dropped from? You don't mean to say that you came after me in spite of all?"

I explained everything to him. At first he looked angry and then he broke into a bitter laugh. "It seems everyone was out watching my wooing." Then he *looked seriously at me. "Did Stapleton ever strike you as being crazy?"*

"I can't say he ever did," I said, surprised.

"I dare say not," said Sir Henry sadly. "I didn't think so either until today. What's the matter with me then? You've lived near me for weeks now, Watson. Tell me straight. Is there anything that would prevent me from making a good husband to the woman I love?"

"I should say not."

"What has Stapleton against me? I've only known his sister these few weeks, but from the first I felt she was made for me, and she, too—there's a light in a woman's eyes that speaks louder than words. But all she would say to me today is that this is a place of danger and she will not be happy until I leave. So I asked her to marry me. Then Stapleton arrived, white with rage. I lost my temper too and botched it all. Just tell me what it all means, Watson, and I'll be forever in your debt."

I could offer no explanation to the poor, down-hearted fellow. However, our questions were set to rest that afternoon by a visit from Stapleton himself. He apologized for his rudeness. He also promised not to object to the baronet's courting of his sister if Sir Henry would go slowly and work on a friendship first. After three months, Stapleton could then feel confident that his sister was not rushing into a rash romance. He and Sir Henry shook hands on this.

That night, Sir Henry and I sat up in his room

until three o'clock in the morning, but no sound did we hear except the chiming of the clock. It ended by both of us falling asleep in our chairs. We decided to try again the following night.

Once more we sat up, not daring to sleep, our senses keenly alert. Then we heard a creak of a step in the passageway. Once the footsteps had passed, we set out in pursuit. We were just in time to catch a glimpse of the tall, black-bearded figure of Barrymore tiptoeing down the hall. We feared the creaking floorboards would give us away. But fortunately, the butler is rather deaf and was concentrating on his mysterious task. As we reached the door of the room, we peeped inside and found him at the windowpane, exactly as two nights ago.

The baronet, always a man who favors direct action, walked right into the room. As he did so, Barrymore sprang from the window. His eyes were full of horror and astonishment.

"What are you doing here, Barrymore?" Sir Henry demanded. "Look here, we'll have the truth out of you, so no lies!"

The fellow looked at us in a helpless way, wringing his hands in misery. "I was doing no harm, sir."

"But then what are you doing with the candle?"

"Don't ask me, Sir Henry," the man begged. "I give you my word that this is not my secret. If it were, I would not keep it from you."

A sudden idea came to me. I took the candle from Barrymore's trembling hand. "He must use it as a signal," said I. "Let us see if there's an answer." I held it to the window as he had done. "There it is," I cried as a pinpoint of light appeared in the black veil of the moor.

"No, no, sir, it is nothing," said the butler.

"Move your light across the window, Watson!" shouted Sir Henry. "See, the other moves also!"

The baronet turned to the butler. "Now, you rascal, speak up. What is going on?"

"It's my business, and not yours," Barrymore said resentfully. "I will not tell."

"Then you must leave my employment right away."

"Very good, sir, if I must."

"And you must leave in disgrace. By thunder, you should be ashamed of yourself," Sir Henry said sternly. "Your family has lived with mine for over a hundred years, and now I find you in some dark plot against me."

"No, no, sir, not against you!" a woman's voice sounded. Mrs. Barrymore stood at the door.

"We have to go, Eliza," Barrymore said firmly. "This is the end. We can pack our things."

"Oh, John, John, have I brought you all this? It's my doing, Sir Henry. He has done this for my sake. My unhappy brother is starving on the moor. We cannot let him die at our gates. Our light is a signal that food will be brought to him. His light is to show us the spot to which we should bring it."

"Then your brother is . . ." I started.

"The escaped prisoner, sir . . . Selden."

"That's the truth," said the butler. "There was never a plot against you, Sir Henry."

The baronet and I stared in amazement at Mrs. Barrymore. She looked steadily at us, and the pain in her eyes was deep. "He is my youngest brother, and we pampered him too much when he was a lad. When he broke from prison, he knew his older sister could not abandon him. So he rushed here straight away. That is the whole truth, and the fault does not lie with my husband, but with me."

"Well," said Sir Henry in a gentle voice, "I cannot blame you, Barrymore, for standing by your wife. Forget what I said. Go to your room, and we shall talk further tomorrow."

When they had gone, Sir Henry and I looked out the window again. The light still glowed.

"How far do you think it is?" I asked.

"Not more than a mile or two," Sir Henry stated. "It can't be far if Barrymore had to carry food there. By thunder, Watson, I'm going to take that man!"

The same thought had crossed my mind. No one would be safe with Selden free. "I'll get my revolver and come with you," I said. In a few minutes, we were outside the door. A thin rain began falling. Yet the light still burned steadily in front of us.

Suddenly, there rose out of the vast moor that strange cry I had heard near the Grimpen Mire. The sound came on the wind—a long, deep mutter, then a rising howl, and finally a sad moan in which it died away. Again and again, it sounded, wild and menacing.

"Watson," cried Sir Henry. "What is it?" There was a break in his voice that showed the sudden horror that had seized him.

My blood ran cold. "Folks around here say it's the Hound of the Baskervilles," I whispered.

"I don't think I am a coward, Watson, but that sound freezes my very blood. Feel my hand!"

It was as cold as marble. "Shall we turn back?"

"No, by thunder!" Sir Henry cried. "We'll get that man even if all the fiends of the pit are loose upon the moor."

We stumbled along in the darkness. We spotted a candle wedged in the crack of a large boulder, and no sign of life near it.

"What shall we do now?" whispered Sir Henry.

"Wait here behind these rocks. Let us see if we get a glimpse of him," I whispered. The words were hardly out of my mouth when an evil yellow face was thrust over the boulder. Foul with mud, matted hair, and a bristling beard, the face might well have belonged to a wild animal.

Sir Henry and I sprang forward. At the same time, the convict leapt over the rocks with the ease of a mountain goat. We were both fair runners, but there was no chance of overtaking him. He was soon lost in the darkness.

The moon was low, and the jagged edge of a granite stone hill stood out clearly against the curve of the moor. The hill was called the Black Tor. There on the Tor, outlined against the shining background of the moon, was a tall, thin man. He stood with his legs apart, his arms folded upon his chest, and his head bowed as if in thought. It was most certainly not Selden. Perhaps in my next letter, I'll be able to shed more light on this stranger. It would be best, however, Holmes, if you could come down and take over my responsibilities.

——— ∽ ———

From this point on, dear reader, I will draw from sections of my diary:

October 16th—A dull, foggy day with a drizzle of rain. It is somber inside the house and out. The baronet is in a black mood after the excitement of last night. I feel danger coming upon us, but I cannot define it. Twice I have heard a sound like the baying of a hound. There must be an explanation. Any hound that cries out in the night and leaves prints in the mud must fall within the laws of nature. And what of the man in the cab, the warning letter, the missing boots, and the man on the Black Tor? If I could lay my hands on him, we might find the end to our difficulties.

After breakfast, the baronet called me into the billiard room, where he was discussing something with the butler. "Watson, Barrymore asks us for his wife's sake not to pursue Selden," declared Sir Henry.

Barrymore nodded. "Arrangements have been made for him to go to South America in a few days," he said. "I give you my word, he will trouble no one. You cannot tell the police where he is without getting us into trouble."

"I guess I couldn't give the man up to the police if what you say is true," Sir Henry admitted. "All right, Barrymore, we give our word."

With a few broken words of thanks, the man turned, but he hesitated and came back. "I should like to do the best I can for you. I know why Sir Charles was at the moor gate that tragic night. It was to meet a woman."

"To meet a woman! He?" the baronet cried.

"Yes, sir. But I know only her initials—L. L."

"How do you know this, Barrymore?" I asked.

"Well, Sir Charles received many letters, for he was known to have a kind heart and a generous hand. That morning there was only one letter, so I took notice of it. It was from the village of Coombe Tracey, written in a woman's hand. Weeks after Sir Charles's death, Eliza was cleaning out his study, and she found the ashes of a burned letter in the back of the fireplace grate. One charred slip could still be read, and it said: 'Please, please, as you are a gentleman, burn this letter, and be at the gate by ten o'clock. L. L.'"

"Have you got the slip?" I asked.

"No," the butler answered. "It crumbled to bits when we moved it. I didn't mention it before this because we found it so long after his death."

"Have you any idea who L. L. is?" Sir Henry asked.

"No, sir. No more than you have."

"Very good, Barrymore." When the butler left, the baronet turned to me and said, "What do you think of this new light?"

"It seems to leave the blackness darker than ever," I replied. "I think we should let Holmes know of this at once. I am much mistaken if this doesn't bring him here." I went to my room and drew up a report.

———— ❦ ————

October 17th—All day long, the rain poured down. I put on my raincoat and walked out upon the sodden moor. God help those who wander into the great mire now. I found the Black Tor safely, but there was no trace of the solitary watcher.

On my way back, I was overtaken by Dr. Mortimer in his small wagon. "Can you think of any woman in the area whose initials are L. L.?" I asked as we jolted along the road.

Dr. Mortimer thought a few minutes. "No one in Grimpen, but there is a Mrs. Laura Lyons who lives in Coombe Tracey."

"Who is she?"

"She is Frankland's daughter."

"What! The old crank?"

"Exactly. She married an artist named Lyons. He proved to be a blackguard, and he deserted her. She's had quite a hard time of it. Since she had married without her father's permission, Frankland has refused to have anything to do with her."

"How does she live?"

"A few of us—Stapleton, Sir Charles, and I—helped set her up in a typewriting business." He wanted to know why I was interested, but I managed to put him off without causing suspicion. I have not lived for years with Sherlock Holmes for nothing.

October 18th—I rose early and told Sir Henry that I should visit Mrs. Laura Lyons alone, because she might be more willing to talk to one person than to two. However, I had some misgivings about leaving Sir Henry alone at the manor.

Reaching Coombe Tracey, I had no difficulty finding someone who would show me the way to Mrs. Lyons's lodgings. A maid showed me in. A woman at a typewriter sprang up with a pleasant smile of welcome. She was indeed a handsome woman. Her eyes and hair were a rich hazel. Her cheeks were colored by a slight flush and a sprinkling of freckles.

"I have the pleasure of knowing your father," I said. It was a clumsy introduction.

"There is nothing in common between my father and me," she stated with hardness in her eyes. *"I owe him nothing. If it weren't for Sir Charles and other kind hearts, I would have starved. State your business."*

"I came to ask about Sir Charles."

The freckles started out on the lady's face. *"What can I tell you about him?"* Her fingers played nervously on her typewriter keys.

"Did you correspond with him?"

Anger gleamed in her nut-brown eyes. *"Why do you ask?"*

"I wish to avoid a public scandal. It is better if I ask you questions than if I pass the matter on to the police."

She was silent, and her face was very pale. Then she declared defiantly, *"I wrote to him once or twice to thank him for his kindness."*

"Have you ever met him?"

"Yes, but only on the few occasions when he came to Coombe Tracey."

"If you knew him so little, how did he know enough about your situation to help you?"

"Several of his friends knew of my difficulties. I believe Mr. Stapleton informed Dr. Mortimer and Sir Charles of my troubles."

"Did you ever ask Sir Charles to meet you?"

Mrs. Lyon flushed with anger again. *"Really, sir, this is a most extraordinary question. No, I certainly did not."*

"Surely your memory deceives you," I continued. "Did you not write, 'Please, please, as you are a gentleman, burn this letter and be at the gate by ten o'clock'?"

It seemed she might faint. But then she recovered herself and gasped out, "Is there no such thing as a gentleman?"

"There is no need to blame Sir Charles. He did burn the letter, but even after burning, a letter is often readable. So you admit to writing the letter?"

"Yes, I did write it," she cried in torment. "Why should I deny it? If you've heard anything of my unhappy history, you know that I made a rash marriage and had reason to regret it. My husband made my life unlivable. Even now I live with the fear that he might get the law to force me to live with him. To gain my freedom, I had to find money for a divorce. So I wrote to Sir Charles, for I felt he might help me if I could talk to him. But I did not want to cause him a scandal. So I wrote the letter in private and asked to meet him in secret. But I never came that night."

"You didn't? Why not?"

"Because I received help from a different source."

"From whom?"

"That is my business alone."

"Why, then, did you not write to him and tell him?"

"I received the good news at the last minute. The next day, I read of his death in the paper."

Her story rang true. If, indeed, she had traveled

to the manor and back to Coombe Tracey that night, someone in the village or at Baskerville Hall would have noticed. But there were still unanswered questions: Did she file for a legal divorce the next day? Who helped her at the last minute? How did she know of Sir Charles's trip to London? Why did she act so secretively? For the moment, I knew I could get no more information from Mrs. Lyons.

I decided to search the moor for the man on the Tor on the trip back from the station. As I was driving past Mr. Frankland's property, he was standing near his garden gate.

"Good day, Dr. Watson," he called out. "You really must give your horses a rest and come have a glass of wine." Though I disliked Frankland, especially in light of his history with his daughter, I took him up on his invitation. One never knows where clues can be discovered. So I sent Perkins back to Baskerville Hall to watch over the baronet.

"Today is a day for congratulations," Frankland said, as he led me into his dining room. "I have discovered the location of the convict on the moor."

I listened intently, shocked that Selden was still near.

"You may be surprised," announced Frankland, "that food is taken to him by a child. I see him every day through my telescope upon the roof."

Here was luck, I thought to myself. Frankland had stumbled upon the man on the Tor. "Indeed, couldn't the child be bringing lunch to a shepherd?"

"Ridiculous!" shouted Frankland. "The Black Tor

is the stoniest part of the moor. It's no place for sheep. Wait," he cried, pointing out the window, "Do my eyes deceive me, or is there something moving upon that hillside? Come, sir, come! You will see with your own eyes and judge for yourself."

He rushed upstairs to the roof, and I followed at full speed. He clapped his eye to the telescope and gave a cry of delight. "Quick, Dr. Watson, before he passes over the hill." Sure enough, there was a small boy with a bundle over his shoulder, toiling slowly uphill, looking around suspiciously.

"Well, am I right?"

I tried to speak in an uninterested tone. "Certainly, there is a boy who seems to be on a secret errand."

"Ah, and now I must swear you to secrecy, Dr. Watson. I will handle this in my own way. But, surely you are not going! We have yet to celebrate."

Somehow I managed to resist his invitation and discourage him from walking home with me. I kept to the road as long as his eyes were upon me. Then I struck off across the moor for the stony Tor. The sun was sinking low, and a thin haze hung in the sky. The boy was nowhere to be seen. The barren landscape of the moor, with its mystery and loneliness, struck a chill into my heart.

As I climbed, I noticed down beneath me, in the cleft of the hill, a circle of stone huts. In the middle was one with a roof sturdy enough to provide shelter against the weather.

An overgrown path among the boulders led to the

*opening. I approached warily. All was silence. At
last, my foot was on the edge of his hiding place—
his secret was in my grasp. My nerves tingled with
the adventure. I closed my hand upon my revolver and
walked swiftly to the opening and peered in. The
place was empty.*

*This was certainly where the man lived, however.
Some blankets rolled in a waterproof tarp lay upon a
slab of rock. Ashes were heaped under a crude fire
grate. There were cooking pots, a bucket of water,
and the child's cloth bundle. In it was a loaf of bread,
a tin can of beef, jars of peaches, and a note. This is
what I saw, roughly scrawled in pencil:*

Dr. Watson has gone to Coombe Tracey.

*It was I, then, and not Sir Henry, who was being
dogged by the secret man. I looked around, but failed
to find any sign of the character of the man who lived*

there. I swore I would not leave the hut until I knew.

Outside, the sun lay on the horizon. I sat in the increasing darkness of the hut and waited. From far away came the clink of a boot striking a stone. Then another, and yet another. I made my pistol ready. There was a long pause. Then once more the steps came closer, and a shadow fell across the opening of the hut.

"It's a lovely evening, my dear Watson," said a well-known voice. "I really think you would be more comfortable outside than in."

Watson has found his mystery man. Does he have enough information now to solve the case and protect Sir Henry? Check the Clues that follow to see if you have noted all the important points. Do you know why and how Sir Charles died? Do you think Holmes has figured it out yet?

CLUES
that will lead to the solution of
The Hound of the Baskervilles

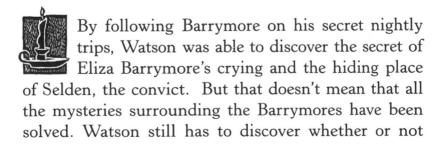 By following Barrymore on his secret nightly trips, Watson was able to discover the secret of Eliza Barrymore's crying and the hiding place of Selden, the convict. But that doesn't mean that all the mysteries surrounding the Barrymores have been solved. Watson still has to discover whether or not

the man who was dogging Sir Henry in London was
wearing a fake beard or a real one.   Does John Barrymore have still another secret hidden?

Miss Beryl Stapleton keeps trying to warn Sir
Henry away from the moor. Watson wonders
why. Does she know something more than
what she says? Her brother keeps a close eye on her,
and she seems frightened of him overhearing her. Why
does he treat her this way? What is wrong?

Mrs. Lyons is the strongest clue. She was sup-
posed to meet Sir Charles that night, but she
didn't. Who stopped her? Dr. Mortimer?
Rodger Stapleton? Her father? Barrymore? Did this
person meet Sir Charles instead? Did he bring a dog
to frighten the baronet to death? Watson knows he
has to find out who Mrs. Lyons's friend is if he wants
to solve this mystery.

Mr. Ian Frankland keeps a close watch on the
moor with his telescope. Why is he so interested in it?   Does he know something more
than the others about the Hound? Did he know about
his daughter's secret meeting?

"*Creep forward quietly and
see what they're doing.*"

THE HOUND
OF THE BASKERVILLES
Part III

For a moment or two, I sat breathless, hardly able to believe my ears. That cold, direct voice could belong to but one man in all the world.

"Holmes!" I cried.

"Come out," said he, "and please be careful with that revolver."

I stooped through the narrow stone opening, and there was Holmes. "I've never been more glad to see anyone in my life," I said as I wrung his hand.

"The surprise is not all on one side, Watson. I had no idea you had found my retreat until I was within twenty feet. When I see a footprint with a bootmark from Bradley, Oxford Street, I know my friend Watson is in the neighborhood. Excellent work, my good Watson. How did you come to find me?"

"Your boy has been seen, and that gave me a lead."

"The old gentleman with the telescope, no doubt. Well, let us see what Cartwright has brought us to eat," said Holmes. "What's this paper? So you have been to Coombe Tracey?"

"Yes, to see Mrs. Laura Lyons."

"Well done! Our searches have been running along parallel lines," said Holmes.

"But how in the name of wonder did you come here?" I asked. "I thought you were in Baker Street on that blackmail case."

"That's what I wished you to think."

"So you use me and don't trust me!" I cried, with some bitterness. "I think that I have deserved better at your hands, Holmes."

"My dear fellow, you have been invaluable to me by thinking I was in London. It threw our opponents off guard and allowed me to gather facts I could not have uncovered if I had been staying at the Hall. I beg you to forgive me for the trick I played upon you. It was best not to take the risk. I brought the lad Cartwright down from London with me to aid me."

"Then my reports have been wasted!" My voice trembled as I recalled the pains I took to write them.

Holmes took a bundle of papers from his coat pocket. "Here are your reports, and they are very well thumbed, I assure you."

I was rather raw over the deception, but I felt in my heart that he had done the right thing. He saw the shadow rise from my face. "That's better," he said. "And now tell me of your visit to Laura Lyons."

As we sat together in the twilight, I told Holmes of my visit and what was said. "This is most important," he said when I concluded. "You are aware, perhaps, that she and Stapleton are involved in a romance?"

"No, I wasn't," I replied.

"Indeed, it is true. They meet and write often.

This knowledge will be a powerful weapon to get his wife on our side."

"His wife?" I asked, utterly confused.

"Yes. Rodger Stapleton is married to the woman he calls his sister."

"Good heavens, Holmes! Are you sure?"

"Quite. He gave you one piece of true information when he told you about himself. He was a schoolmaster in the north of England, and there is nothing easier to trace than a schoolmaster. A man of his description and his wife started a school that closed under shameful circumstances. This man was an avid pursuer of butterflies."

"I see, it all falls into place," I said. "But what could be the purpose of all these lies?"

"Stapleton must feel it is more useful for himself and his wife to appear free. No doubt, Laura Lyons seeks a divorce to marry Stapleton."

All my vague suspicions suddenly took shape. I saw the naturalist as something terrible—a creature of much patience and craftiness, with a smiling face and a murderous heart. "What will Laura Lyons think when she finds she has been betrayed?" I asked. "And Sir Henry! He has fallen in love with Mrs. Stapleton."

"It will be painful for all," Holmes agreed. "But our greatest duty to Sir Henry is to protect him. Don't you think, Watson, that you have been away from your charge too long? Your place is at the Hall."

Night was settling upon the moor. A few faint stars were gleaming in the violet night. "One last question, Holmes," I said as I rose. "What is the meaning of it all? What is he after?"

Holmes's voice sank as he answered. "Murder, Watson. Cold-blooded, deliberate murder. Do not ask me for more now. My nets are closing upon him even as his are closing upon Sir Henry. But until then, you must guard Sir Henry as a mother watches her sick child. Hark!"

A terrible scream—a yell of horror and anguish—burst out over the silence of the moor. That frightful cry turned my blood to ice in my veins. "Oh, my God!" I gasped. "What is it?"

"Hush!" he whispered. "Hush!"

Now the cry burst upon our ears, nearer, louder, more urgent than before."

"Where is it?" Holmes whispered; and I knew from the shrill in his voice that he, the man of iron, was shaken to the soul. "Where is it, Watson?"

"There, I think." I pointed into the darkness.

Again the agonized cry swept through the silent night, louder and nearer than ever. A new sound now mingled with it—a deep, muttered rumble, a growl rising and falling like the low murmur of the sea.

"The Hound!" cried Holmes. "Come, Watson, come! Great heavens, if we are too late!" He ran swiftly over the moor, with me at his heels. In front of us came one last despairing yell and then a dull, heavy thud. We halted and listened. Not another sound broke the heavy silence of the windless night.

I saw Holmes put his hand to his head like a man

lost. He stamped his feet. "He has beaten us, Watson. We are too late."

"No, surely not!"

"Fool that I was not to act. And you, Watson, see what comes from abandoning your charge. If the worst has happened, by heaven, we'll avenge him."

Blindly we ran through the gloom, forcing our way through bushes and panting up hills. At every chance, Holmes looked eagerly around him, but the shadows were thick and nothing moved. Then a low moan fell upon our ears. To our left, there was a ragged ridge of rocks. As we came to it, we saw that it dropped down into a sheer cliff. Below it, on a jagged rock, was a dark, irregular object. We ran around the ridge to the bottom. There was a man lying on his face, his head crushed and crumpled at a horrible angle. Not a whisper or rattle came from him.

Holmes lighted a match. As it shone, our hearts turned faint and sick within us—it was the body of Sir Henry. Neither of us could mistake the peculiar ruddy suit he had worn the day we first met him. The match flickered out as hope went out of our souls.

"The brute! The brute!" I cried with clenched hands. "Oh, Holmes, I shall never forgive myself for having left him to this fate."

Holmes groaned. "I am more to blame than you, Watson. But how could I have known he would go out on the moor against my warnings? Stapleton shall answer for this, Watson. He has killed the uncle and now the nephew. But it is not what we know. It's what we can prove to the law. If we make one false move now, he might escape us."

"What can we do then?"

"We can do right by our friend, here, and wait for morning." Holmes bent to move the body. Suddenly he was dancing and laughing and wringing my hand.

"Good heavens, are you mad?" I shouted.

"A beard! A beard! This man has a beard!" His joy knew no bounds.

"A beard?" I was lost.

"It is not Sir Henry, Watson—why it must be my neighbor, Selden, the convict!"

With feverish haste, we turned the mangled body
over. There was no doubt. It was indeed the face that
had glared upon me through the candlelight. In an
instant, it was all clear to me. Barrymore had passed
the old clothes of Sir Henry off to Selden, to help him
escape. The tragedy of Selden was black enough, but
at least the convict had already been facing death for
his crimes. I explained to Holmes why Selden was
wearing Sir Henry's old clothes.

"But why should the Hound be loose tonight?"
Holmes asked. "Stapleton would not let the Hound
loose unless he thought Sir Henry would be here. And
what is it about the Hound that makes one man die
of fright and another run to his death? Halloa, Watson,
what's this?" Holmes whispered. "I do believe it is the
man himself. Not a word now to show what we suspect or my plans shall crumble to the ground."

A figure was approaching. I could tell it was the
dapper shape and jaunty walk of the naturalist. He
hesitated when he saw us, then came on. "Why, Dr.
Watson, that's not you, is it?" said Stapleton. "But,
dear me, what's this? Somebody hurt? Don't tell me
it is our friend Sir Henry!" He brushed past and
stooped over the dead man. I heard his sharp intake
of breath.

"Who's . . . who's this?" he stammered.

"It's Selden, the criminal who escaped from Princeton Prison," I replied.

Stapleton turned toward us. Not a sign of disappointment showed on his face. "Dear me! What a

shocking affair. How did he die?" he asked.

"He appears to have fallen over this ridge of rocks and broken his neck," I said. "My friend and I were taking a stroll on the moor when we heard his cry."

"That brought me over this way too. I was uneasy about Sir Henry. I had asked him to come over. When he did not arrive, I came out to see if he was on his way, and I was alarmed by the screams. By the way, did you hear anything else? You know the stories the local people tell about the Hound. I wonder if it appeared tonight."

"We didn't see it or hear it," said I.

"Then, Mr. Holmes, what is your theory of this poor fellow's death?" Stapleton asked, smiling. "We have been expecting your arrival since Dr. Watson came down. Your fame makes it hard for one not to recognize you."

"Unfortunately so at times," Holmes replied. "In this tragedy, I could have done nothing. The cold and loneliness must have addled this man's brain. I dare say he rushed about in the dark until he broke his neck. This ends a thoroughly unsatisfactory case. I return to London tomorrow."

Stapleton looked hard at my companion. "Then you have not been able to shed light on the mysterious happenings that have puzzled us all?"

"Indeed not. An investigator must have facts, not legends and rumors," Holmes answered frankly.

Stapleton asked us to visit him, but we resisted the invitation. The three of us covered the convict's body, and then Holmes and I set off for Baskerville Hall.

"We're at close grips at last," said Holmes. "Say nothing of the Hound to Sir Henry, Watson. Let him believe just what we have told Stapleton. It will help him face what lies ahead."

——— ∽ ———

Sir Henry was more pleased than surprised to see Holmes. He *did* raise his eyebrows, though, at the fact that Holmes had no luggage, nor any explanation why it was missing. While Holmes chatted with the baronet, it was my task to break the sad news to John and Eliza Barrymore. It was distressing, and the poor woman wept bitterly into her apron. I left the Barrymores to share their grief in private.

At dinner, Holmes and I explained to Sir Henry the fate of the criminal Selden. We did not mention the growling of the Hound or Stapleton.

"But what of the case?" Sir Henry asked Holmes. "Watson and I are not much wiser than when we came down from London. We've heard the Hound on the moor, though, so we can swear that it's not all empty ghost stories. If you can put that beast on a chain, I'll swear you are the greatest detective of all time."

"I think I'll chain him all right if you will give me your help," said Holmes.

"Whatever you tell me to do, I will do."

"Good, but you will have to do it without asking the reason," Holmes warned.

"Just as you like."

Suddenly Holmes stopped what he was about to say and stared at the air over my head.

"What is it?" Sir Henry and I cried at once.

I could see Holmes was holding down some unusual emotion, and his eyes were lit with amused triumph. "Please excuse the admiration of an art critic," he said calmly. "These are really fine portraits. They are all family portraits, I presume?"

"Every one," Sir Henry answered, puzzled.

"Do you know their names?"

"Barrymore has been coaching me. The gentleman with the telescope is Rear Admiral Baskerville, who served under Rodney. The man in the blue coat is Sir William Baskerville, who served in the House of Commons."

"And the Cavalier? The one in the velvet and lace?"

"Ah," said Sir Henry, "that's the wicked Hugo, the cause of the evil curse of the Hound. We're not likely to forget him."

"Dear me!" said Holmes. "He seems quiet and mild-mannered enough, but I dare swear, there's a lurking devil in his eyes."

The picture of Sir Hugo fascinated my friend, for his eyes were continually flying back to it during dinner. Later, when Sir Henry had gone to his room, Holmes led me back to the dining hall with a lighted candle in his hand. He held it up next to the portrait of Sir Hugo. "Do you see anything there?"

I looked at the plumed hat, the dangling curls, the white collar, and the straight, severe face.

"Is it like anyone you know?"

"There's something of Sir Henry about the jaw."

"Wait an instant," whispered Holmes. He jumped on a chair, and holding the light in his left hand, he curved his other arm over the broad hat and ringlets.

"Good heavens!" I cried in amazement. The face of Rodger Stapleton sprang from the canvas.

"Ha, you see it now," said Holmes.

"This is marvelous. It might be his portrait."

"Yes. The fellow is a Baskerville, no doubt of it. This picture supplies us with our missing link. Before tomorrow night, Stapleton will be fluttering in our net like one of his butterflies." As he jumped down, Holmes burst into one of his rare fits of laughter.

— ⟿ —

The next morning I was up early, but Holmes was afoot earlier still. I found him in the dining room, dressed in his outdoor clothes and staring at the portrait of Sir Hugo. "Watson, the nets are all in place. We'll soon know whether we have caught him or he has slipped through our meshes."

"What have you done?"

"First, I let my young friend Cartwright know that I'm safe, and then I notified the police about Selden."

"What is the next move?"

"To see Sir Henry. Ah, here he is."

"Good morning, Watson, Holmes," said the baronet pleasantly. "You look like a general planning a battle."

"That is the exact situation," agreed Holmes. "Watson was just asking for orders. I believe you are engaged to dine with the Stapletons tonight."

Sir Henry smiled. "I hope you will come also. I'm sure you would be welcomed."

"I'm afraid that will be impossible, Sir Henry. Watson and I must go to London."

"To London?" Sir Henry stared at us in shock and disappointment.

"Yes. We should be more useful there at this time."

"I had hoped you would see me through this business," Sir Henry groaned. "The Hall and moor are not pleasant places when one is alone. Perhaps I should also take a trip to London."

"You have promised to trust me and do as I ask," Holmes replied sternly. "It is essential that you remain here and act naturally. Let your host know that urgent business called us to London. However, do not worry, we shall be back in Devonshire very soon."

"Very well, then," said Sir Henry. "When do you propose to leave?"

"Immediately after breakfast," said Holmes. "Watson, you must send a note of regret to Stapleton. Sir Henry, one more thing. I wish you to drive to Merripit House. But then send Perkins back and walk home by yourself."

"Across the moor?" Sir Henry frowned. "You've always warned against it."

"Yes," said Holmes. "But this time you may do it in safety. If I had not every confidence in your nerve and courage, I would not suggest it. But, as you value your life, keep to the path that leads from Merripit House to the Grimpen Road."

I was most astounded by Holmes's plan, but this was no time to question him. After a quick breakfast, we bade good-bye to our disgruntled friend. A few hours later, we were at the train station of Coombe Tracey, where we found the lad Cartwright waiting.

"Any order, sir?" the boy piped up.

"Take this train to London. When you purchase your ticket," said Holmes, giving the boy some money, "ask if there is a message for me."

Shortly afterward, Cartwright returned with a telegram. Holmes handed it to me. It ran: *Wire received. Coming down with an unsigned arrest warrant. Arrive five-forty. Lestrade.*

"I felt we should have Inspector Lestrade here so

that all goes smoothly and within the law. Until he arrives, we can call upon Mrs. Laura Lyons."

We found her in her office. Holmes opened his interview by speaking frankly. "I'm investigating the death of the late Sir Charles Baskerville," said he. "My friend here, Dr. Watson, has told me about the information you kept hidden about this matter."

"What information?" she asked defiantly.

"We know you asked Sir Charles to be at the gate on the evening and hour of his death."

"There is no connection between those events."

Holmes leaned forward in his chair. "Mrs. Lyons, this is a murder case. Any information we have may affect Stapleton and his wife."

"His wife!" she cried, jumping out of her chair. "Rodger is not a married man!"

"It is no longer a secret," Holmes said. "The woman who passes for his sister is his wife."

"Prove it! Prove it!" The fierce flash of her eyes said more than any words.

"I am prepared to do so," Holmes replied, drawing papers from his pocket. "Here is a photograph of Mr. and Mrs. Vandeleur taken in a York school four years ago. I'm sure you will recognize them. Here are reports from three trustworthy witnesses who knew the couple when they were at St. Oliver's School."

She glanced at the photograph, then looked up at us with a desperate face. "Mr. Holmes, this man asked me to marry him if I could get a divorce from my husband. He has lied to me, the villain. Why? Why?

One thing you must believe, I never dreamed harm would come to the old gentleman, for he was one of my kindest friends."

"I entirely believe you, madam," said Holmes. "So it was Stapleton who suggested that you send the letter to Sir Charles."

"Rodger told me what to write, word for word."

"I presume that he suggested that you ask Sir Charles for money to pay for your divorce. And then, as you were about to leave, he pressured you into breaking the appointment."

"Exactly. And he frightened me into silence."

"I think," said Holmes, "that you have had a fortunate escape. He knew you had information that could harm him, and yet you are still alive. The threat to your life shall soon be under lock and key. But for now, Mrs. Lyons, we must say good morning."

———— ✑ ————

We lunched in a slow fashion and then went to wait for the train from London. At five forty-two, Inspector Lestrade, a thin, wiry bulldog of a man, sprung from the train. "Anything big?" he asked. After working with Holmes on a number of cases, Lestrade had come to look at him with a kind of awe.

"The biggest thing in years," said Holmes.

We had at least two hours to wait before the action would start, so we found a pub and filled Lestrade in on the details of the case. Sherlock Holmes, however, did not reveal his plans for the evening. I could only deduce what our course of action might be.

My nerves thrilled with anticipation when at last we were upon the moor road with the cold wind blasting against our faces. Every turn of the wheels took us nearer to our supreme adventure. A short way from Merripit House, we paid our driver and started to walk.

"Are you armed, Inspector?" asked Holmes.

"As long as I have trousers, I have a pocket. And as long as I have a pocket, I have something in it. What's the game now?"

"A waiting game. Walk on tiptoe, and do not talk above a whisper." About two hundred yards from the house, Holmes put up his hand. "This will do. These rocks make an admirable screen. Watson, you have been in the house, what's the room behind those shuttered windows?"

"Those are the kitchen windows, and the one with the bright light shining from it is the dining room."

"Creep forward quietly, and see what they're doing." I crept along in the shadow of the low garden wall until I could look through the uncurtained window. Stapleton was talking excitedly, but the baronet looked pale and worried. Beryl Stapleton was not in sight.

Soon Stapleton rose and left the room. Sir Henry remained, picking at his dinner. I heard steps pass on the other side of the wall where I crouched. Once the footsteps passed, I looked over and saw Stapleton. He was holding a boot in his hand and unlocking the door of a toolshed. A weird scuffling sound came

from within. Stapleton entered and stayed inside only
a minute or so. Then he relocked the door and made
his way back to the house. I returned to my waiting
companions and told them what I had seen.

"You say the lady is not there?" asked Holmes.
"Where can she be? There's no light in any room
but the kitchen."

"I cannot imagine," I replied.

Behind the house, a great, dense white fog hung
over the Grimpen Mire and was slowly drifting in our
direction. The first thin wisps of it were curling across
the golden square of the lighted window. Holmes
muttered impatiently as he watched the fog's sluggish
drift. "It's moving toward us, and that's serious. Sir
Henry's life depends upon his coming out before the
fog is over the path."

The light in the kitchen suddenly shut off. It
seemed the servants were leaving. Every minute, the
white cloud drifted closer.

"Shall we move back up the path to higher ground?"
I asked Holmes.

"Yes. That would be our best chance," Holmes
answered, cursing the crawling fog. As it flowed
toward us, we kept moving back until we were now
almost a half mile away from the house. Still the
dense white sea crept onward.

"We have gone back far enough," said Holmes.
"We dare not chance missing him."

A sound of footsteps broke the silence on the moor.
The steps grew louder, and through the fog stepped

the very man for whom we were waiting. Sir Henry was walking swiftly and kept looking back over his shoulder. He didn't see us as he passed and went up the long slope behind us.

"Hist!" cried Holmes, as he cocked his pistol. "Look out! It's coming."

A crisp, continuous patter rushed toward us from Merripit House. I glanced at Holmes for a second. His face was pale and tense, his eyes shining brightly in the moonlight. Suddenly, his lips parted in amazement, and his eyes widened into a fixed stare.

At the same instant, Lestrade gave a yell of terror and dropped face downward upon the ground. I sprang to my feet, but the hand grasping my pistol went limp. My mind was struck actionless.

A dreadful shape sprang upon us from the shadows of the fog. A hound it was, an enormous coal-black hound, but not a hound such as any mortal eyes have ever seen. Fire burst from its open mouth. Its smoldering glare stood out of glowing circles. Its muzzle, shoulders, and chest were outlined in flickering flame. Never in the nightmarish dream of a disordered brain has anything more savage, more appalling, more hellish been imagined.

With long bounds, the huge, black creature followed hard upon the footsteps of our friend. So shocked were we all that it passed before we recovered our nerves. Then Holmes and I fired together, and the creature gave a hideous howl. One of the shots had hit him.

The animal did not pause, but bounded onward. Yet with that howl of pain, the Hound had blown away all our fears. If he could be wounded, he was not a ghost. As we flew down the path, we heard the deep roar of the Hound and scream after scream from Sir Henry. I never saw a man run as Holmes ran that night. He outpaced me as I outpaced Lestrade.

Just as I rushed up, the Hound sprang upon the baronet, hurled him to the ground, and went for his throat. The next instant, Holmes emptied five rounds of his revolver into the creature's flank. With a howl of agony and a vicious snap in the air, it rolled over on its back, its feet pawing furiously. Then it fell limp upon its side. The giant Hound was dead.

Sir Henry lay unmoving beside it. We tore away

his collar, and Holmes breathed a prayer of thanks when he saw no signs of a wound. Our friend's eyelids quivered, and he made a weak effort to move.

"What in heaven's name was it?" he whispered.

"It's dead, whatever it was," Holmes said in a gentle, soothing voice. "We've laid the family ghost to rest once and forever."

Even in death, the Hound was an incredible creature. It appeared to be part bloodhound and part mastiff—as gaunt and powerful as a small lioness. The huge jaws dripped with a bluish flame. I placed my hand upon the glowing muzzle, and as I pulled back, my own fingers gleamed in the darkness. "Phosphorus," I noted.

"A cunning preparation of it," said Holmes. "It doesn't have a strong smell that might distract the dog." Holmes knelt beside the baronet. "We owe you a deep apology, Sir Henry, for exposing you to this danger. I was prepared for a hound, but not for such a creature. And the fog gave us little time to act."

"You saved my life," Sir Henry said weakly.

"Are you strong enough to stand?" I asked.

"If you help me up, I shall be ready for anything. What do you intend to do?" Sir Henry tried to stagger to his feet, but failed. We helped him sit on a rock.

"Sir Henry, you are not fit for further adventures tonight," Holmes directed. "We will leave you here briefly. In time, one of us will return to help you back to the Hall. The case is solved, and now we want our man."

Holmes, Lestrade, and I walked swiftly back to Merripit House. "It's a thousand to one against finding him here," said Holmes. "Those shots told him the game was up, but we'll search to be sure."

The front door was open, and we rushed in. There was no one in the lower rooms. Upstairs, however, Lestrade heard someone moaning behind a locked door. Holmes struck the door with the flat of his foot, and the door flew open.

The room was like an old museum. Dead butterflies in glass jars lined the shelves along the walls. In the center of the room was an old upright beam. Tied to this post was a figure wrapped up and muffled in sheets. Two dark eyes, filled with grief, shame, and anger, stared at us. In a minute, we tore off the bonds, and Beryl Stapleton sank to the floor. Along the side of her neck was a red welt made by a whip.

"The brute!" cried Holmes, rushing to the aid of Miss Stapleton.

As we helped the woman to a chair, she gasped, "Is he safe? Has he escaped?"

"He cannot escape us, madam," said Holmes.

"No, no," she said frantically. "I mean Sir Henry. Is he safe?"

"Yes. And the hound is dead."

"Thank God! Thank God! Oh, this villain! See how he has treated me." She shot her arms out from her sleeves, and we saw with horror that they were mottled with lashes and bruises. She broke into passionate weeping.

"Where can we find him?"

"There's only one place where he could have fled," she answered. "There is an old tin mine in the heart of the mire. He would fly there."

The fog lay white against the window. Holmes held the lamp toward it. "No one can find his way in the Grimpen Mire tonight."

She laughed, and her eyes and teeth gleamed with fierce merriment. "Rodger may have found his way in before the fog covered it, but he'll never find his way out," she said. "He planted guiding wands in the mire to guide his way. Oh, if only I could have plucked them out today, you would have had him at your mercy."

"It was you who sent Sir Henry the warning note in London," Holmes stated.

"Yes. I tried to warn him away," cried the woman. "I've had no proof that my husband did harm to Sir Charles. But I knew how he was treating me and that poor, half-starved hound. So I suspected he had a part to play in the old gentleman's death. I didn't want another innocent person to be drawn into his clutches! I tried to say something more to Sir Henry, but my husband never left us alone. He knew better than to do that!" Then she broke down into another fit of sobbing. It was clear that it would take her a long time to heal from the nightmare she had lived.

Lestrade remained at the house with Mrs. Stapleton while Holmes and I went with the baronet to the Hall. This night's adventure had shattered his nerves. We sent Barrymore for Dr. Mortimer.

The next morning, the fog lifted. Mrs. Stapleton guided us to the point where the marked pathway through the bog began. The trail zigzagged from tuft to tuft of rushes through the bog. More than once, a false step plunged us thigh-deep into the dark, quivering mire. When we sank into it, it was as if some evil hand were tugging us down into the black depths.

Only once did we see a sign that someone had passed before us. On top of the slime, a dark shape rested. Holmes stepped off the turf to get it and sank to his waist. Had we not been there to drag him out, he would never have set foot on firm soil again.

Holmes had found a boot, and *Meyers, Toronto* was printed on the leather inside. "It's Sir Henry's missing boot," Holmes shouted, waving it in the air. "Stapleton must have dropped it as he ran away. At least we know he came this far in safety."

But more than that, we were not fated to know. When we reached the firmer soil of the bog island, we saw no trace of Stapleton's footsteps. We could only suppose that somewhere in the heart of Grimpen Mire—down in the foul slime that sucked him in—this cold and cruel-hearted man is forever buried.

In the abandoned cottages near the tin mine, we found chains and gnawed bones. It was clear that this was where the hound had been kept. Off to the side, we found a tin of glowing phosphorus paste.

"It was a clever device," said Holmes. "I say it again, Watson, that we have never yet hunted a more dangerous man than the one who is lying yonder." Holmes swept his long arm toward the huge mottled expanse of green-splotched bog.

—— ∽ ——

When we returned to London, Holmes did additional research on the character of Stapleton. As he had suspected, Rodger Stapleton was actually the son of Rodger Baskerville, Sir Charles's youngest brother. This brother had fled to Central America, where he had married and had a son—Rodger Baskerville, Jr. As a young man, Rodger, Jr., had married Beryl Garcia, from Costa Rica. Then he stole some money and came back to England, posing as Rodger Vandeleur, a schoolmaster. After the scandal at the school, the Vandeleurs changed their names and came to Devonshire. Rodger had discovered that there were only one or two people between himself and the Baskerville fortune. He forced Beryl to act as his sister. Since Beryl had no family in England and no money to return to Costa Rica, she was trapped.

When Rodger Baskerville arrived in Grimpen, he made friends with Sir Charles. He heard from the baronet about the legend of Sir Hugo and the Hound. That's when his cunning plan was hatched. He went to London to buy the largest, most frightening hound he could find. He was able to trick Laura Lyons into luring Sir Charles out to the moor gate on that trag- ic evening. Rodger dressed the massive hound up in phosphorus and let him loose next to the gate. He chased Sir Charles till the man died of fright and a heart attack.

When Rodger heard about Sir Henry, he took his wife to London to spy on his rival for the fortune. He stole Sir Henry's boots for future use. He was prevented from doing anything more dangerous be- cause Sherlock Holmes had been called into the case.

No one is quite sure how Rodger Baskerville planned to lay hold of the family fortune once he killed Sir Charles and Sir Henry. Holmes thought he prob- ably would have returned to South America. There he could have made a claim to the money without ever returning to Baskerville Hall.

Thus ended one of the longest and most frighten- ing cases of Holmes's career. Sherlock's greatest regret was that Sir Henry had to go through such shock and pain. To recover from his shattered nerves, the baronet decided to take a cruise around the world. To the young man, the saddest part of all this black business was that Beryl had tricked him. Yet before Sir Henry left on his trip, he gave money to Holmes so Beryl might return to her family in Costa Rica. It would not shock me to hear that in the later course of his travels, Sir Henry decides to visit this small country.

As you tramped through the muck and mire of the moor, were you able to pick up the last of the clues? Just examine the **Clues,** *and see how well you followed the case. This will help you prepare for the next adventure of Sherlock Holmes and his friend Watson.*

CLUES
that led to the solution of
The Hound of the Baskervilles

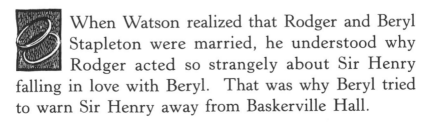

Holmes and Watson shared notes and discovered that Stapleton had been meeting Laura Lyons, and Mrs. Lyons had had an appointment to meet with Sir Charles the night he died. Holmes and Watson then knew that Stapleton was the prime suspect.

When Watson realized that Rodger and Beryl Stapleton were married, he understood why Rodger acted so strangely about Sir Henry falling in love with Beryl. That was why Beryl tried to warn Sir Henry away from Baskerville Hall.

Holmes stared at the portrait of Sir Hugo on the wall and saw Rodger Stapleton's face. Holmes remembered that Dr. Mortimer had said that Sir Charles's youngest brother was the picture of the wicked Hugo. Holmes figured that Stapleton wanted to kill Sir Henry to inherit the Baskerville fortune.

Holmes wanted to catch Stapleton with his hound and in the act of the crime. So he made Sir Henry think that he had returned to London. In this way, Stapleton wouldn't suspect he was being watched.

Stapleton took Sir Henry's old boot to the tool-shed. It was then obvious that Stapleton stole the two boots at the hotel. He stole the new one by accident and returned it because it didn't have any of Sir Henry's scent on it. Stapleton needed the old boot to get the hound to chase after Sir Henry.

When Holmes and Watson discover the real-life hound, they find him covered with a phosphorus paste. With this glow-in-the-dark paste, Stapleton had made the dog seem fierce, ghostly, and larger than life. This explains why the dog could scare Sir Charles to death and chase Selden off a cliff.

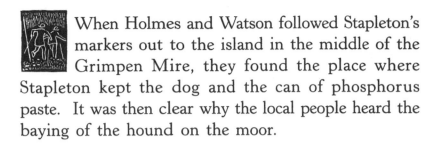When Holmes and Watson followed Stapleton's markers out to the island in the middle of the Grimpen Mire, they found the place where Stapleton kept the dog and the can of phosphorus paste. It was then clear why the local people heard the baying of the hound on the moor.

The ENGLAND of Sherlock Holmes